For Aidan and Fay ~ L J
For Roo, and not forgetting Murphy ~ A E

Copyright © 2008 by Good Books, Intercourse, PA 17534
International Standard Book Number: 978-1-56148-635-9

Library of Congress Catalog Card Number: 2008003047

Text copyright © Linda Jennings 2008
Illustrations copyright © Alison Edgson 2008
Original edition published in English by Little Tiger Press,
an imprint of Magi Publications, London, England, 2008.
Printed in China

Library of Congress Cataloging-in-Publication Data

Jennings, Linda M.

Little puppy lost / Linda Jennings ; illustrated by Alison Edgson.

p. cm.

Summary: When three puppies go out for their first romp in snow, they are
frightened by a stranger and Ollie, separated from his siblings, must try to
find his way home through snowy fields and icy woods.

ISBN 978-1-56148-635-9 (hardcover : alk. paper)

[1. Dogs--Fiction. 2. Animals--Infancy--Fiction. 3. Snow--Fiction.
4. Lost children--Fiction.] I. Edgson, Alison, ill. II. Title.

PZ7.J429849Lit 2008

[E]--dc22

2008003047

Little Puppy Lost

Linda Jennings

illustrated by Alison Edgson

Good Books

Intercourse, PA 17534
800/762-7171
www.GoodBooks.com

Ollie peeped out of the barn door. Something cold and wet plopped on his nose. "What's all this white stuff, Mom?" he squeaked. "Can we eat it?"

"It's snow, Ollie," his mom laughed. "It falls like rain in winter. And no, you shouldn't eat it."

"Can we play in it, then?" he asked.

"Please, Mom," cried Sheba and Sam.

"Of course you can," said Mom, "but don't go too far."

Sam and Sheba skidded and slid
across the icy farmyard.
"Wait for me!" yelped Ollie,
racing after them.

When the puppies reached
the field, they stopped and stared.
There was snow everywhere.
  "Let's play!" cried Ollie.

The puppies chased and dug
and rolled under the flying
snowflakes, until
suddenly . . .

. . . a strange face loomed up in front
of them – a face with a huge mouth,
huge eyes and a HUGE bark!

For a moment the puppies
froze with fear.
"RUN!" Sheba cried.

The puppies rushed off through the flurrying snowflakes. Ollie's paws scrabbled and skidded as he ran and ran, until at last the dog's barks faded and everything was quiet and still. But where were Sheba and Sam? Where were the farmyard and the barn?

"Oh no," whimpered Ollie.
"I'm lost!"

"Too whit,

too whoo,

who are you?"

hooted a voice high above him.
Ollie looked up. Two big, round
eyes stared down.

"I'm Ollie and I've lost my family
and I don't know my way home,"
Ollie squeaked.

"Perhaps you should follow your
footprints," suggested the owl.
"They'll lead you home again – but
hurry, or they'll be covered in snow."

"Thank you so much!" said Ollie.
"I'll do that."

Tail wagging, he set off. But by the time
he had reached the middle of the field, the
footprints were disappearing under fresh
snow. Soon Ollie couldn't see them at all.

He trudged on and on as the snow grew
deeper. "I must keep going," he panted.
"I *must* get back to my nice, warm basket
and supper."

At last Ollie reached the edge of the woods. Were these the woods by his farm? If they were, then he was nearly home!

The snow had stopped falling, and
evening sunlight shone through the trees.
Crunch, crunch, Ollie crept through
the icy leaves. But then, all at once . . .

Swoosh!

Ollie slipped down
an icy slope,

tumbling

over

and over . . .

THUMP!

From the shadow of the bushes
three fox cubs stared out at him.

"Look what the snow's blown in,"
said one.

"What a scruff!" said another.

"This is *our* home," said the third.
"Clear off!"

"But I don't know which way to go!"
cried Ollie. Sadly he walked away. He
would have to find his own way home.

Ollie reached the edge of the woods, but still he couldn't see the farm. He tried to cheer himself up. He'd have so much to tell Sam and Sheba when he reached home!

But the snow was falling once more, thicker and faster. As he struggled on, Ollie began to think he would never see his family again.

Cold, hungry, and very, very tired, Ollie crawled under a bush.

A mouse scurried past his feet and disappeared into a small hole. "I wish I could find somewhere safe and warm to sleep, too," Ollie sighed. But as he closed his eyes, he heard something . . .

"Ollie! OLLIE! Where are you?"
Ollie peeped out from the bush –
it was Mom!

"Mom! Sam! Sheba! I'm over here!"
And across the frozen field Ollie
raced to meet them.

"We've been looking for you for hours," cried Mom. "Where have you been?"

"I've had an adventure," said Ollie. "But I'm so glad it's over now."

"So am I," said Mom, gently licking his freezing ears.

Home at last, Ollie curled up with his brother
and sister in their cozy bed. The puppies wanted
to know all about Ollie's snowy adventure.

"Tell us more about the owl!" cried Sheba.

"And the nasty fox cubs!" squeaked Sam.

But, warm and snug, his tummy full of dinner,
Ollie had fallen fast asleep.